Birthday Cake!

First published in 2009
by Wayland

Text copyright © Louise John
Illustration copyright © Miriam Latimer

Wayland
338 Euston Road
London NW1 3BH

Wayland Australia
Level 17/207 Kent Street
Sydney, NSW 2000

Series Editor: Louise John
Cover design: Paul Cherrill
Design: D.R.ink
Consultant: Shirley Bickler

A CIP catalogue record for this book is available from the British Library.

ISBN 9780750259392

Printed in China

Wayland is a division of Hachette Children's Books,
an Hachette UK Company

www.hachette.co.uk

Birthday Cake!

Written by Louise John
Illustrated by Miriam Latimer

WAYLAND

Mum went to the supermarket.

Poppy went too.

"We need some sugar,"
said Mum.

"I can get it," said Poppy.

"We need some flour, too," said Mum.

"I can get it for you," said Poppy.

"I can get the butter," said Poppy. "It is up here."

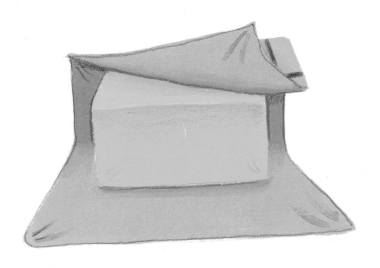

"The jam is here,"
said Mum.

"I can get it for
you," said Poppy.
"Here you are."

"We need a box of eggs," said Mum.

"Oh, no! I can't get it!"
said Poppy.

"I can get it for
you," said Mum.
"Here you are!"

Poppy and Mum
went home.

"Now we can make a
cake!" said Mum.

19

"Happy Birthday, Dad!"
said Poppy.

Happy Birthday

21

Guiding a First Read
Birthday Cake!

It is important to talk through the book with the child before they read it alone. This prepares them for the way the story unfolds, and allows them to enjoy the pictures as you both talk naturally, using the language they will later encounter when reading. Read them the brief overview, and then follow the suggestions below:

The high frequency words in this title are:
can   for get here I it Mum said some the to we   went you

1. Talking through the book
It was Dad's birthday, so Poppy helped Mum to find everything they needed at the supermarket to make a cake for him.

> **Let's look at the title page of** Birthday Cake.
> **Show me what they need to buy to make the cake.**
> **Turn the page. So Mum and Poppy went – where?**
> **That's right, the supermarket.**
> **On page 6, Mum said, "We need some… ?" Yes, sugar.**

Continue through the book, guiding the discussion to fit the text, as the child looks at the illustrations.

> **Look at page 16. Oh dear! Poppy can't get the eggs.**
> **"Here you are," said Mum.**
> **Turn the page. Now what are they going to do?**
> **And what do you think Poppy said to Dad on the last page?**

22

2. A first reading of the book

Ask the child to read the book independently and point carefully underneath each word (tracking), while thinking about the story.

Work with the child, prompting them. Praise their careful tracking, attempts to correct themselves and their knowledge of letters, sounds and punctuation, for example:

> **Good reading. You made that sound just like Mum and Poppy talking together.**
> **You said, "Oh no! I can get it." Does that make sense? Try it again, looking carefully and thinking about the story.**
> **Say 'butter' again slowly and look at all the letters in the word.**

3. Follow-up activities

· Select two high frequency words, and ask the child or group to find them throughout the book. Discuss the shape of the letters and the letter sounds.

· To memorise the words, ask the child to write them in the air, then write them repeatedly on a whiteboard or on paper, leaving a space between each attempt.

4. Encourage

· Reading the book again – with expression.

· Drawing a picture based on the story.

· Writing one or two sentences using the practised words.

START READING is a series of highly enjoyable books for beginner readers. **The books have been carefully graded to match the Book Bands widely used in schools.** This enables readers to be sure they choose books that match their own reading ability.

Look out for the Band colour on the book in our Start Reading logo.

The Bands are:

Pink Band 1

Red Band 2

Yellow Band 3

Blue Band 4

Green Band 5

Orange Band 6

Turquoise Band 7

Purple Band 8

Gold Band 9

START READING books can be read independently or shared with an adult. They promote the enjoyment of reading through satisfying stories supported by fun illustrations.

Louise John is really the editor of Start Reading, but wanted to see how she liked writing books, too. It was quite tricky, but she found that eating lots of chocolate biscuits made her think better! She tries out her ideas on her daughter, Amelia, who tells her if they are any good or not!

Miriam Latimer enjoys illustrating and writing stories for children. She carries her sketchbook and pens with her everywhere she goes, which make her handbag very heavy. She likes to sketch people in cafés and train stations but, if they notice, she pretends to be drawing something else!